THE BUTTI
LADY ANI

GW00859288

REV]

"A magical fantasy story full of adventure that keeps you hooked from the beginning. The vibrant illustrations bring the characters to life and pop from the page. A great read!"
FFION JONES, Author of 'I GIVE YOU THE MOON'

Fans of epically magical stories, you have found your next go to book. This is a fantastic story of myth and magic, all wrapped up in a love letter to wildlife and nature, complete with charming illustrations. A terrific Tolkienesque tale of folklore and fantasy. A masterclass in world building and fables that will leave you buzzing for the next one...
CHRIS WHITE, Author of 'S.H.E.L.L. (Episode 1) THE HORSE AWAKENS'

Ig Oliver's "The Butterfly Bee Lady and the Bee" is a beautiful and idyllic tale of the wonder of nature. It instils in the reader a clear evocation of nature coupled with a vibrantly engaging tale, which will delight and enthral readers. The talented author not only tells the tale but also illustrates it with some entrancing and delightful pictures, which perfectly complement the prose.
IAN BILLINGS, Author of 'BILLY PLONKA AND THE GROT LABORATORY'

THE BUTTERFLY BEE LADY AND THE BEE

IG OLIVER

Ventorros Press

THE BUTTERFLY BEE LADY AND THE BEE
ISBN Print: 978-1-7399528-4-6
ISBN eBook: 978-1-7398334-1-1

Copyright © Ig Oliver 2017
Illustrations © Ig Oliver 2015
This version © Ig Oliver 2022
This edition © Ventorros Press Limited 2022
Facebook: The Butterfly Bee Lady
The right of Ig Oliver to be identified as the author and illustrator of the Work has
been asserted him in accordance with the Copyright, Designs and Patents Act 1988
Web Site: www.ig-oliver-author.com
Facebook: facebook.com/IgOliverChildrensAuthor
Twitter: @ig_author
Instagram: instagram.com/IgOliverChildrensAuthor
Published by Ventorros Press 2022
Web Site: www.ventorrospress.com
Facebook: facebook.com/Ventorros
Twitter: @VentorrosP
Instagram: instagram.com/ventorrospress
Set by The Logical Choice, Newquay, Cornwall, UK
Printed by TJ Books, Padstow, Cornwall, UK
Cover illustration by Ig Oliver © Ig Oliver 2022
Cover Design by Chris White

To my daughters Farhanna and Indiana

ACKNOWLEDGEMENTS

I would like to thank all the local Northwood and Derbyshire businesses who have supported THE BUTTERFLY BEE LADY AND THE BEE, as well as the many reviewers who have written amazing, honest appraisals.
To my family, who supported my decision to originally write my original story and then continue the tale; my partner Anita and our daughters, Farhanna and especially Indianna, who first instigated the idea of telling the story.
Acknowledging all the many others who have supported me throughout my journey; my friends, and of course Graham Mulvein of Ventorros Press who has always believed in my work.

Was it the thought to write that changed us?
Or was it the thought that we should.

Ig Oliver

1.

A long time ago... about the time my mother was eight years old, in a garden in the countryside, there lived a beautiful Butterfly who referred to herself as the Butterfly Bee Lady, but that wasn't her real name. She spent her summer days buzzing around the meadows and paddocks, flying between the trees and the flowers.

She had the most beautiful wings, full of colours like a spring rainbow; but nature had worked a strange magic on her and she truly believed that she was a Bee, a belief fuelled by the fact her dress was patterned with black and yellow stripes.

One day she was fluttering through the daisies, when she came across an actual big round Bee that was collecting nectar from the flowers. His pockets were obviously bulging with yellow pollen powder and he looked extremely busy.

"Hello'z," said the Bee Lady, as she landed on a daisy, which bent and wobbled as she came to rest.

"Hello'z," replied the Bee, who immediately stopped what he was doing and turned to face the Butterfly.

Drawing out his hanky, which was covered in pollen, making a puff of yellow cloud as he did so, he wiped the sweat from his brow. "How'z can I'z help you'z?" he said with a big smile.

"Oh," replied the Bee Lady, "I just thought I'd come over and see how you were doing. As a fellow Bee, I thought I might be able to help!"

The Bee looked at her with a surprised, wide-eyed expression. "Err—"
He was about to mention the fact that she wasn't actually a Bee, when
she continued...

"Isn't it a lovely day for collecting pollen?" she said, as she started
stuffing some yellow dust into her striped pant pockets.

"Err... yez," said the Bee, looking slightly bemused. He did not want
to appear rude by mentioning the fact that she was in actual fact
a Butterfly, and not a Bee; although a rather strangely dressed
Butterfly, he had to admit.

She had on a yellow and black striped outfit, which simply didn't match
her beautifully coloured wings. But being a very polite Bee, he really
didn't want to appear rude or impolite; and in any case, this Butterfly
seemed very nice. She had a gentle, kind face and had even tried to
speak in Bee language, by adding 'z's to her words, which he found
quite amusing.

"Yez, it'z a beautiful day for collecting pollen; it'z warm and dry'z, just perfect. The best day so far this summer," the Bee continued, raising his eyebrows. Then he asked politely, "Sorry, I didn't catch you'z name. My name is Bramley," he added.

"Oh, I'm so sorry," said the Butterfly with a bright smile, "I didn't introduce myself properly. My name's Bee Lady." She promptly fluttered to the ground and curtsied in front of the Bee called Bramley.

Bramley smiled at her and bowed in return. "The pleasure iz all mine." he said as he stood up straight.

The rest of the day, the two unlikely looking new friends spent time chatting and collecting pollen, until the sun turned a deep red and started to sink down to set behind the trees and hills.

"Will you be here tomorrow, Bramley?" asked Bee Lady.

"Oh yez, I'z be here. There's still lot of work to be done before the summer comes to an end."

"Wonderful," replied Bee Lady, "Okay, I'll see you tomorrow," and as she did, she lifted gracefully into the air, waved, and was gone.

2.

Over the next few weeks, Bramley and Bee Lady met up in the garden every day. They spent the days collecting pollen, chatting, flying amongst the flowers, catching the warm breezes under their wings, meeting with other friends and having lots of fun.

Bramley was so happy to have Bee Lady as his new friend. She was always joking and playing tricks on him and making him laugh. He found it so funny when she spoke in Bee, but he never once mentioned to her that she wasn't really a Bee, he was far too polite.

Then one day, for no reason, Bee Lady didn't appear and Bramley was a little sad, as she had not told him she wasn't coming to the garden that day. She was usually up bright and early to meet him. Bramley thought that maybe she was a little tired, or maybe he had simply not heard her mention that she wouldn't be around that day. So he carried on with his duties, although it was nowhere near as eventful or fun as when Bee Lady was about.

The next day, Bee Lady did not appear again and Bramley became a little concerned. So he asked a few friends whether they had seen her but none could say that they had.

"Maybe she's gone on holiday!" said Mr Weevil, who was dragging large sacks of flour through his front door, stopping for a moment to rub his long snout, "Or maybe she's visiting family!"

"Yez, possibly," said Bramley, as he buzzed his wings harder and rose above the grass. "Well, if you should see her, let her know I was looking for her," he shouted, as he rose higher and higher.

Bramley spent the following week worrying about his friend as there'd been no sign of her, but he had to keep working and collecting pollen for the hive, as collecting pollen was very important. He occasionally asked passers-by and acquaintances if they had seen the Butterfly Bee Lady with the yellow-striped dress, but no one had.

On the eighth day, Bramley was loading his pollen into a wheelbarrow, when he suddenly heard a voice behind him that he recognised.

"Hello'z, Bramley," said the voice.

He turned around and there she was, fluttering and hovering behind him, smiling as the sun twinkled in her eyes. At first, Bramley tried to hide his happiness at seeing her as he was more than a little annoyed, as she had left without saying anything; but in the end he couldn't resist it any longer; he was simply too happy to see her.

He buzzed over to her, put his arms around her and hugged her, and said, "I mizzed you'z! Where did you'z go?"

Bee Lady looked at him and smiled. "It's a long story, Bramley. Maybe I could tell you over a cup of honey tea, or maybe, if you have time I could take you and show you."

"Show'z me?" asked Bramley.

"Yez!" Bee Lady said, "Maybe it would be better to show you," she replied.

Bramley thought for a moment, but only a short moment. "Yez, okay, I'z come with you."

Bramley followed Bee Lady; happy to know she was okay. Bee Lady waved him on. "Let's go'z!" she said.

They rose up together through the tall, scented bluebells, cowslips, clovers and dandelions and sped off, whipping through the leaves on the trees, catching the breeze towards the distant meadows.

After a while, Bee Lady stopped by a large tree, surrounded by buddleia flowers, lilacs, sage, marjoram and tall sunflowers, growing all around it. The scent of the flowers filled the air with beautiful aromas.

Bramley settled on the branch of the big tree, breathed in deeply, and filled his lungs with the wonderfully aromatic air. He looked towards Bee Lady, who was staring up into the tree with her beautiful smile.

"So," Bramley said softly, "Iz thiz what you wanted to show'z mee'z?"

Bee Lady's wings fluttered slightly and then her eyes rested once again on Bramley. "Yez," she replied smiling, "I'm sorry I disappeared without saying anything but something happened, something wonderful! It was very sudden in the morning and I couldn't leave my home...my tree."

Bramley looked intrigued, "Wonderful?" he asked.

"Yez," said Bee Lady, as she raised her eyes upwards, towards a large green leaf dangling just above their heads.

Bramley slowly followed her gaze, up towards the leaf.

"My'z babies!" Bee Lady whispered.

Bramley stared at the leaf, his eyes suddenly focused on a small cluster of golden-yellowy eggs with stripes on. He then blinked and stared even harder... and after a moment, he said, "You'z had babiez?"

"Ninety-one babies, to be exact!" Bee Lady said, with a little giggle in her voice.

They both continued to stare up to the leaf for a while, both with different thoughts, until Bramley eventually spoke. "Well, I'z understand now why you'z disappeared. But I'z so happy you'z came back and brought me'z to this place. I'z realize why you'z home is here. It'z so beautiful and such a nice tree to raise your family in!" he said.

Bee Lady moved closer to Bramley, smiled and took his hand in hers.

"You are a good friend, Bramley," she said, "You are honest, I love you dearly, and I trust you. I'm so sorry I disappeared, but I had to and now I must leave again." Her eyes saddened as she spoke. "I have to go away."

"Go'z away again?" Bramley repeated, staring at her, unbelieving, suddenly feeling alarmed, unsure of what she meant.

"Yes, Bramley, I have to take a journey; a long journey, a long, long journey... It's crucial you understand and can help me."

Bee Lady stopped as a tear dropped from her eye and landed on Bramley's hand. He stared down at it.

9

"I must go. It's difficult to explain. I wouldn't go unless I had to. It's very important and I just need you to trust me; to understand."

Bramley shook his head slowly in disbelief, looking down at the tear in his hand and then back up into Bee Lady's face, his eyes filled with sorrow. For now he understood.

"You'z not coming back, are you'z?" he said.

"I need you to watch over my'z children and keep them a secret," Bee Lady said, still clutching his hand.

"Visit when you can, just to make sure they're safe. I know you're a good Bee, and they'll need a good Bee to guide them."

Bramley didn't know what to say; he hovered silently, shocked at the unexpected revelation. And then as a gentle wind rustled the leaves around him, he said, "I'z never done this before. I'z wouldn't know what to do'z? Why do you'z have to go'z?"

Bee Lady smiled, "When the time comes, you'll know. You'll only have to pass by and check that they're okay."

As she said this, she leant forward and kissed Bramley on his forehead and whispered, "I have to go, Bramley, I have to go now." She fluttered her wings and rose up towards the leaf where her eggs lay and pulled some golden pollen out of her pocket.

Bramley had never in his life seen golden pollen before. He watched as she whispered something and then blew gently on her hand; the pollen then rose and flew upwards, coating the eggs.

"But'z, but'z…" Bramley stuttered, "don't go'z, pleaze don't go'z!"

Bee Lady looked down on Bramley as she fluttered her wings, moving backwards, ever further away, "I must go'z… Thank you, Bramley, thank you. I trust you!" At this, she suddenly spun around, her wings now fully open, caught an unexpected breeze and was gone.

Bramley flumped backwards, and sat on the branch, stunned at what had just happened, emotions running wildly through his mind; anger, confusion and loss. He pulled out his hanky and blew his nose; a cold chill came over him as the sun crept behind some clouds. He stared out through the shady leaves of the tree, across the fields into the distance, lost in thought and sadness.

The next morning when the sun was barely up, Bramley sat on the edge of an old millstone, which was used as a sundial in the garden, his mind not on the day's work which still lay ahead. He was missing his friend, Bee Lady. His emotions were still in shock. He was worried about why and where she had gone and why she had left in such a hurry?

Finding himself the sole custodian of ninety-one baby eggs he felt entirely alone. He needed some good advice, so he thought, *there's only one person who might be able to help and that I can fully trust; whom all Bees trust, the Queen.*

Getting an audience with the Queen was going to be tough; he had to have a really good reason.

Suddenly, he remembered the gold pollen Bee Lady had taken from her pocket and blown on her eggs. "Yez," he said out aloud, "I'z must go'z back and collect some of the gold pollen, and show the Queen. I'z sure she has never seen anything like it before." He stopped suddenly, realising he was talking to himself out loud. He quickly looked around to see if anyone was listening but it was all right, he was alone. Bramley jumped up, buzzed his wings and headed back towards the great tree.

He flew near to the eggs, making sure no one was watching. The eggs had grown larger and the leaf had begun to sag under the weight. He looked carefully around to see if there was any pollen but it had seemed to have all disappeared. Then unexpectedly, out of the corner of his eye, he saw five small grains lying on the edge of the leaf.

Bramley carefully brushed them all onto his hand and as he did so, they glowed like twinkling diamonds containing all the beautiful colours of a rainbow. Luckily, he had an old envelope in his pocket with his time sheet in. He placed the pollen inside, smiled to himself and set off back to work.

Later that day, when all the heavy work of pollen harvesting was over, Bramley made his way back to the hive. He scribbled his name on the back of the envelope and looked inside to make sure the golden pollen was still there, but was shocked to see there was one missing. He could only find four pieces. "Oh dear!" he mumbled to himself, "It must have dropped out while I was working."

He checked his pockets but nothing; *No time to look now*, he thought to himself. He sealed the envelope and buzzed over to the great hive door. Standing at the entrance was the Guard Bee, looking incredibly smart and formal.

"Bramley," said the Guard, "What can I'z do for you'z?" Looking extremely stern as he spoke, he squinted one eye, to add to the effect. Bramley buzzed up closer.

"I'z have a letter for the Queen," he said; "It'z very important. Can you'z get it to her for mee'z?"

The Guard laughed, "Ha! Iz it you'z resignation, Bramley? Haz you'z decided to harvest better pastures?"

"Err... no'z," said Bramley, "It'z just a letter. Can you'z pleaz get it to her?"

The Guard frowned slightly and looked down at Bramley. He knew him and he knew that he was an honest hard-working Bee. After a few seconds, he said, "Mmmzz... I'z do my'z best. You'z go'z home now and let mee'z see what I'z can do."

It had been a long hard day. Bramley felt very tired and so went home to rest and have a nap, but no sooner had he put his head on his pillow, than there was loud banging on his door. He jumped up startled, wondering who could be making so much noise. He went over to his door and opened it. To his surprise and shock it was the Bee Guard he had given the letter to, accompanied by six other Guards.

"Bramley," the Guard said, in a commanding voice, "You'z must come with uz immediately. The Queen has demanded you'z come straight to the hive."

Bramley had been envisaging meeting with the Queen, but this was not quite how he had imagined it might be.

He was told to wait alone in the imposing throne room at the back of the hive and not to touch anything, by one of the Queen's Hive Superintendents. So he sat in silence. He was beginning to wonder whether he had done the right thing by presenting the golden pollen, when suddenly the big doors at the end of the throne room swung open. The Queen entered followed by the King, who was small, with a grey beard and spectacles. The Queen was much, much bigger!

They were followed by an entourage of officials and busy looking Bees. The Queen and King sat on their thrones and stared for a moment at Bramley.

"Are you'z the one'z who'z sent this envelope?" said the Queen, holding it up in front of Bramley, "Are you'z Bramley?"

Bramley bowed in front of his Queen, feeling more than a little worried. He managed to shakily buzz the words out of his mouth. "Yez, your Majesties."

The Queen looked at the Bee before her; "Tell mee'z, how you'z came by these?" she asked with a very uncompromising, Queen-like voice.

The King latched his glasses over the end of his nose and peered over them. Bramley took a deep breath and nervously started to tell the Queen and King how he came to have the pollen in his possession.

"My'z good friend, Bee Lady," he said nervously. "She'z..."

"Bee Lady?" interrupted the Queen curtly. "What Bee Lady?"

Bramley then hurriedly started to explain that Bee Lady was his friend who actually thought she was a Bee, who dressed in a yellow-striped outfit. The Queen and King turned and stared at each other with surprised expressions.

"Stop'z!" the Queen shouted brusquely to Bramley. She then turned to everyone in the room and immediately ordered them all to leave.

Bramley and the Queen and the King were now alone in the throne room. The Queen and King turned slowly back towards him. This time, it was the King who spoke, "Are you absolutely sure? Tell us the whole story of how you'z came by this golden pollen," the King commanded.

So, Bramley retold the story of how he had met Bee Lady, who was actually a Butterfly; how they became friends; her disappearance, her return; and again, her parting; and how she had asked him to watch over her eggs, her babies; and how he had seen her blow the golden pollen from her hand.

"And these babiez eggs are where?" asked the Queen.

Bramley stopped for a moment, remembering what Bee Lady had asked of him. *Keep them secret, I trust you!* He had promised to keep the eggs safe and secret. The Queen looked at Bramley, sensing that he was struggling to answer her question.

"No, don't tell uz," the Queen said unexpectedly, "It'z of no'z great concern to uz. They're now you'z responsibility. You'z are now their guardian. You'z have been chosen!"

Bramley stared at the King and Queen with questioning eyes. "Chosen?" he nervously asked.

"Yez," said the King, "Chosen! You'z have been chosen. It'z a great privilege."

"I'z don't understand," said Bramley.

The Queen went back to her throne in the corner and sat down. "Let me tell you'z a story'z, Bramley. A very old story'z, from a time long past."

The King put his hand on Bramley's shoulder and gently guided him to a seat, and they both sat down.

"What I'z about to tell you, Bramley, iz a story handed down over many generations and iz steeped in myth and legends," the Queen said, "...only a few have ever heard it before.

"Before the land, sea'z, rivers, tree'z and creatures were as we know'z them today," the Queen began, "there waz only one'z kind of creature, which flew with wing'z. They were called the Dragonflyers and their kind lived everywhere. They ruled the skie'z. Their Queen'z were very beautiful."

"Their Queen'z..." Bramley interrupted.

"Yes, Queen'z," the King answered.

The Queen coughed and said, "Let mee'z continue. Their Queen'z were in fact twin sisters, who'z jointly ruled over their lands. Their names were, Sindeena and Belliza.

"One'z day, Belliza found a beautiful stone, which resembled a crystal; inside it was full of golden pollen, which glowed like the stars.

The Queen'z had both heard stories of such a stone. Belliza believed it was there to protect and fill lives with happiness. But Sindeena believed it held the secret to beauty, long life, and should never be'z shared. One day, the two Queen'z sisters argued over the stone and how it should be used."

The Queen continued, "Sindeena tried to grab the stone from her sister, but as she did so'z, Belliza fell to the floor and the stone'z shattered into millions of pieces, and the golden pollen engulfed Belliza, covering her all over. When the pollen settled, Belliza's wings were covered in the broken crystals, and she couldn't wipe the golden pollen from her clothes. Sindeena, in her fury, lied to everyone, and accused her sister of destroying the precious stone. She said that her sister had been disfigured as a curse for destroying it. She had Belliza sent away; banished never to return. Though secretly, Sindeena had managed to pick up some of the golden pollen from the floor and save it for herself, thereby extending her life. As time went by, flying creatures started to appear that had never been seen before; Butterflies, Bees, Flies and many other creatures with wings."

The King added, "It was believed that Belliza had returned and was coating the eggs of the Dragonflyers with the gold pollen and changing the babies within."

The Queen resumed, "Realizing this, Sindeena then proclaimed her sister as an `Evil Witch` who should be hunted down by all Dragonflyers. On hearing this, Belliza changed her name and managed to disguise herself by using the pollen to change her own appearance. However, by doing this, it changed the appearance of her own offspring forever, giving them alternative lives and Belliza's essence was transferred to them. Of course, no one really knows what happened to Belliza. Some say, she is reborn in a never-ending life cycle; some say, she died at the hands of assassins; but these stories have been told and retold over many generations. And so, the story goes." said the Queen.

"It has always been believed that Belliza iz still around today, or at least one of her descendants iz. And now you come to me and tell me you'z story of the Bee Lady and show me'z the golden pollen. I'z can only believe now that she exists and you'z were chosen to care for and be the guardian of her children, as others have been chosen before you'z," she continued, "You'z must return and fulfil the request of Bee Lady, Bramley. Sindeena's proclamation still exists and all of Belliza's children will always be hunted, too. You'z must watch over them and keep them safe until they're old enough to fend for themselves."

The Queen rose slowly from her throne, pushing the envelope with the remaining golden pollen into her pocket.

"I'll keep this safe, Bramley. We don't want it falling into the wrong hands."

"Go'z now, with our blessing, you'z are free of any obligation to the hive until this job is complete. Return when it's done, I'z may have some other work for you'z."

The King and Queen then left the throne room, leaving Bramley with his thoughts.

3.

Bramley went home.

He gathered some of his belongings and wrapped them up in some old muslin. Then he tied it to a stick and dropped it on his shoulder, locked his front door and headed for the big tree.

It was getting dark and rain clouds had suddenly started to gather over the valleys.

As Bramley approached the large old tree, the grey clouds had a yellow tint to them. He knew from experience that this colour would bring flashes of light and loud thunderous noises.

He settled on the branch near to where he knew the eggs were hidden under the leaf and gazed around.

"I'z sure this was the place," he whispered to himself, as a worried look appeared on his face and he started to buzz around, looking under the leaves.

Bramley kept searching, but he couldn't find the leaf, it simply wasn't there anymore. A sense of dread began to fill his head.

Without warning, the wind began to strengthen and there was a sudden thump sound, as a raindrop hit a leaf next to him. Bramley started to feel dread with the thought that he had lost the eggs, and the words from his Queen echoed through his head, "Fulfil... Chosen guardian..."

Maybe the leaf has fallen to the ground, thought Bramley. He swiftly descended to the bottom of the tree and frantically started to search among flowers and plants.

Thump! Thump! The rain came faster and the wind very quickly grew stronger, whistling around the tree.

Bramley found himself being pushed and thrown about by the whirling wind. He began to shout in the hope he could be heard. "Eggs... Babiez!" he yelled.

The grass and flowers began to bend and sway in the wind, and he began to struggle to fly forward, being constantly pushed back by the wind.

The rain poured down now and started hitting him hard as the weather turned into a storm. Bramley realised it was hopeless to

keep searching. He stared up at the tree swaying above him, its leaves shiny, wet and dripping. For a moment in the howling wind, he thought he heard a voice, "Here, Bramley..." like a whisper, lost in the wind.

He looked above to where he thought the sound had come from and spotted a small hole in the tree trunk. *It's no good'*, he thought, *I have to get undercover.* So, Bramley buzzed his tiny wings as hard as he possibly could and made for the hollow; just managing to grab the bark around the outside of the cavity, he pulled himself through with the last of his strength, landing inside with a bump.

4.

Inside, it was soft and dry and Bramley slowly managed to pull himself up to rest his hands on the rim of the hole to gaze outside. A flash of lightning suddenly blinded his eyes and he stumbled backwards into the darkness.

There was another loud bang and rumble of thunder. He realised he was totally exhausted and so lay there and listened as the rain beat down outside... then unexpectedly, for just a moment, he thought he heard a sound of children whispering with frightened voices... and then, silence once more.

Dazed, Bramley believed the sounds were the wind playing tricks on him. He sat up and gazed out of the hole at the lashing rain and the leaves being battered and blown. Repeatedly, the lightning struck outside. Inside the hole illuminated and once again, Bramley believed he heard whispering coming from behind him. He quickly swung around, but the hole was totally thrown into darkness once more and the sound fell silent.

"Who'z there?" Bramley shouted. There was no answer; so again, he called out, "Who'z in here? I'z know you'z there!"

Silence...

Again, lightning lit the cavity, this time illuminating ninety-one terrified, shivering baby caterpillars, cowering in a corner near the far end of the hole.

Instantly, the whispering started over and the baby caterpillars tried to retreat further into the darkness until they could retreat no more. Bramley now understood that these were Bee Lady's lost eggs. They had hatched, thankfully not lost. A sudden feeling of relief engulfed him.

"It's alright," Bramley said in a calm, reassuring voice, "Don't beez afraid. I'z...I'z your guardian, it's okay, don't be frightened!"

A small female voice came from the group of huddled caterpillars. "Are you our mummy?"

"Uh... no," said Bramley, "I'z your..."

"Daddy..." came the small voice again.

But before Bramley could reply, a small yellow and black striped girl-caterpillar appeared in the light and looked up to him and smiled.

Bramley stared down at her; he'd seen a smile like that before, and he gazed around as more small caterpillars came out of the woodwork into the light, all of them different colours, all looking for reassurance.

"Yes," said Bramley, "Yes...I'z your daddy."

The storm clouds began to recede and the rain abated to light single drops here and there on the leaves outside. A ray of sunlight gleamed through the breaking clouds onto the tree and warm air flowed gently into the hole.

"I'm hungry!" a tiny voice came from the huddled caterpillars.

"Me too!" said another. The small, yellow-striped caterpillar gazed up at Bramley.

"We're all hungry," she said, shuffling up closer to Bramley, followed closely by the other ninety colourful caterpillars, all echoing the same sentiments of hunger.

"Well..." Bramley spoke quickly, trying to think of a way to stop the sudden surge of bodies, "there's plenty to eat outside."

"Outside?" they all whispered in unison, some of them peering out of the hole.

"Outside?" repeated the girl's voice. Bramley noticed the yellow and black striped caterpillar-girl had now moved next to him, watching all the other caterpillars trying to compete for a good viewing point to peer out of the hole. She slowly raised her hand and held his and smiled again.

"Are you going to stay with us?" she asked. "And look after us?"

Bramley nodded, "Yez, I suppose I'z am." He looked around the hole;
it was dry and warm. *I'z could make this a nice home, with some
improvements*, he thought to himself.

"Can we eat now?" asked the caterpillar-girl.

Bramley stared at her and bent down closer to her. "Do you'z have a
name?" he asked.

"Of course I do," she giggled. "What's your name?" she said, staring
back up at Bramley.

Bramley smiled and replied, "My'z name's Bramley Bee."

"That's a nice name...You can call me Bee!" she said, letting go of his hand

and scurrying off to the hole to gaze outside with the others. As she did, she shouted, "The food's outside, is it?" turning back to look at Bramley.

"Yez, at the bottom of the tree!" shouted Bramley, as she disappeared over the edge of the hole, promptly followed by ninety of her siblings.

As the days passed, Bramley got to know his new family. He spent lots of time making the hole habitable and arranging it so that all ninety-one caterpillars had a place to sleep. He'd even found time to make himself a guitar, which he loved to play before bedtime.

Every day some of the growing caterpillars would come up to him to ask him to give them a name. This was the most amusing task; he loved putting names to faces as they all had different characters and they were all happy with whatever name he gave them.

He gave them names of trees, like Ash, Willow, Oakly, Spruce, Elm, Maple and Holly. Some, he gave names of flowers, like Rose, Dandelion, Daisy and Buttercup. Herb names were popular: Basil, Thyme, Sage, Burdock, even Borage. Bramley noticed that for each of the namings, the caterpillar-girl called Bee would stand next to him listening and nodding her head in agreement to each one.

He also noticed each day how the caterpillars grew quickly and spent most of their day eating. They came back to the hole in the evening with big bellies and then huddled up, ready to listen to one of Bramley's tales, or sing songs, mostly about a Bee's life.

The warm air flowed gently. The sun was bright and lit up the big old tree with its rays shimmering through its leaves. Bramley was resting against a branch, strumming his guitar, and feeling happy, as everything was well. It was a wonderful feeling; he was enjoying his life. He'd sit and daydream but in the back of his mind, he still missed Bee Lady, their friendship and her funny ways; and he still wondered where she had gone, or whether or not he would ever see her again.

Bramley's mind drifted as he gently strummed his guitar and dreamt. His dream took him to another world, a world where everything was beautiful. Blue skies filled with yellow-gold sun, where he and Bee Lady flew together, flying through the flowers and grassy paddocks, and all the creatures danced as he played and sang and flew into his dream:

> *Drum, drumz, drumz,*
> *De drum, drum, drumz*
> *(Bramley plucks his guitar),*
> *Sitting here amongst the dandelions.*

A shadow of a Dragonflyer's wings suddenly filled the sky, but slowly transformed to Bee Lady's wings, flying closer. She appears before Bramley smiling.

> *Can you hear the breaze*
> *Flowing through the leave'z*
> *While the sun's beams are*
> *Stroking the land*
> *Gently with its golden hand*
> *And you and me together?*

They fly together through fields and trees, and all the insects, birds and animals sing along:

Flying hand in hand
Let us bee together forever
In this wonderful land
Let us bee together forever
In this golden hand
The wind blows north to south
And east to west
But my'z love for you will always stay true
Forever together
My'z honey it's true, I love you
And as I gaze into this land
I see myself becoming part of you
I'm changing, I'm growing,
It's that golden hand pointing the way
For us to stay
Together forever
Forever together

Abruptly, Bramley was awoken from his dream. Bee was shaking Bramley's shoulder.

"Wake up, Daddy."

She had grown some more. Her bright golden-yellow appearance always shone out. She was quite a funny child and in many ways, reminded Bramley of Bee Lady.

He'd noticed that all the other caterpillars always listened to her whenever she spoke, and he also enjoyed the fact that she asked him lots of questions, to which he'd always try and give an answer.

"Bramley," Bee said, "I want to tell you about a feeling I've been having recently; and it's not just me, it's all my brothers and sisters too. We've all been feeling very tired the past few days." She yawned, even as she spoke, "It's like we all keep stopping and dreaming and then waking up very quickly, but it's been happening more than ever today," she yawned again, "I think something is going to happen to us."

Bramley looked at her and noticed that she did appear tired. "Maybeez you'z all going down with a cold, perhaps you'z should all come in and rest," he said, now a little concerned.

Bee agreed, so she and Bramley called to all the other caterpillars to come home and have an early evening. Bramley got them settled and decided that what they needed was some nice warm honey and pollen from the eucalyptus.

"I'z going to the hive and I'z bring you'z all some nice honey," he told everyone, "I'z be back before the sun goes down."

Bee came over to him and took his hand, "We're going to be all right, Bramley. You don't have to worry about us."

Her face had changed over the past few days, from that of being a baby to a teenager, and she had that smile that Bramley had seen before, a kind of knowing smile.

"You go and get us some nice honey, and when you get back, we'll be ready for a nice long story!" Bee said, smiling again, "Go now, hurry, and don't get lost!"

Bramley laughed, "Tut," he said, "A Bee'z getting lost? I'z never live it down." And off he buzzed.

*****

Bramley struggled to carry the two buckets of honey he'd managed to get from the hive. Having to get honey for ninety-one caterpillars wasn't as easy as he had thought. The buckets were heavy and hurt his fingers and he had to keep stopping to catch his breath and rest his arms. So on the way back, he decided to make a quick detour and pop over to his house and get his work gloves.

To Bramley's horror when he arrived, he found his front door shattered and his entire home broken up, decimated.

He felt angry and saddened all at the same time. *Who or what could have done this to my home?* he thought.

Bramley placed the buckets of honey on the floor of his ruined house, and went immediately to locate his neighbours. He quickly buzzed around to see if anyone was about. Straightaway, he spotted Mr Froghopper's door wide open. He gently popped his head in and instantly saw that everything had been destroyed inside here too.

"Hellozl" Bramley called, "Are you'z here?" There was no answer. He moved to the next nearest house, where Mrs. Woundwort lived. Again, the house was empty, the interior all smashed. Bramley worriedly called out again, but nothing, no reply. *This is terrible*, he thought. *I'll try Rosemary Beetle. She's always in.* Bramley nipped his head through Mrs. Beetle's open door and called out, but there was no reply. Her house looked as though a whirlwind had passed through it. *Where iz everyone?* Bramley anxiously wondered, now very worried.

All of a sudden, he saw old Mr Hairy Snail crawling slowly through the long grass below. Bramley swooped down and landed directly next to him. Mr Hairy Snail instantaneously disappeared inside his shell, as though very scared of something. Bramley knocked gently on his shell.

"Helloz, Mr Hairy. It'z mee'z, Bramley Bee."

"Go away," came a voice echoing from within.

Bramley got himself down as low as he possibly could to see if he could peer into the shell. "It's mee'z, Bramley Bee," he repeated, "You'z neighbour. Where are you'z going? Where iz everyone, Mr Hairy? What's happened?"

Slowly, apprehensively Mr Hairy's long, stalk-like eyes appeared from within the shell and gazed up at Bramley.

"They came..." he replied, his voice still echoing from inside the shell.

"Who came?" asked Bramley, "Who came?"

Mr Hairy's face finally appeared from inside the shell, looking extremely upset, scanning the skies above him. He then frowned up at Bramley.

"They came! They were looking for something, or somebody. Everyone ran. They... they started destroying and breaking everything... we were so scared!"

"Who came, Mr Hairy?" Bramley reiterated.

"The Dragonflyers..." said the old snail, hurriedly slipping back into his shell... "The Dragonflyers came!" his petrified voice echoed from within.

Bramley's thoughts immediately rushed back to the tale the Queen had told him about the Dragonflyer twin sister Queens and the decree Sindeena had issued to hunt down all of Belliza's offspring. He swiftly sensed a cloud of doom cover his head. How and why had Dragonflyers destroyed his home? Nobody knew what he was doing. Nobody except the King and Queen of the hive.

Bramley gazed around watching as Mr Hairy Snail sped off as fast as he possibly could into the undergrowth, and a sad silence drifted across the ruined homes. It was starting to get dark. Bramley knew he had to get back to the tree immediately. Did the Dragonflyers now know where the baby caterpillars lived?

He instantly flew up into the air and headed as fast as he conceivably could to the tree, leaving the buckets of honey behind.

As Bramley approached the old tree, the sun had already settled behind the distant hills and a deep blood-red glow drifted across the horizon. He landed on a nearby branch and slowly looked around. There was no sign of Dragonflyers. None at all. He gazed up at the cavity in the trunk of tree; there was an eerie stillness about it. His heart felt heavy. Was he too late?

Bramley took a deep breath, counted to three, buzzed his wings and flew up to the hole. He hovered in front of it and tried to peer into the darkness. He could neither see nor hear anything. Carefully pushing himself forward into the hollow, he landed gently on the soft moss floor, his eyes desperately trying to focus in the dark.

"It's mee'z, Bramley," he whispered, "Where are you'z?"

No answer.

His eyes strained in the dark and again he called out.

"Where are you, my'z children? It's mee'z... Daddy."

Silence.

Bramley's arms and legs felt weak and his eyes began to water. *I've lost them!* he thought.

Suddenly, there came a small faint voice in the darkness
"Bramley Bee..?"

Bramley strained his ears, sure he had heard something.

Again, came a tiny voice. "Daddy..?"

Bramley turned to where he thought the sound came from and moved gradually forward as his eyes started to focus in the dim light. There, in the depths of the tree hole, he spied Bee's face. His heart pounded as he hurriedly flew over towards her.

"Bee, you'z okay..! You'z okay! You'z hanging upside down, what's happening? Where are the children?"

Bee smiled a gentle smile at Bramley, "You're late," she said softly, "Where's my honey?"

"Bee!" Bramley said, moving closer to her face, "Where are the children?"

Bee smiled once more, and this time her gaze moved from Bramley's face and looked high up towards the interior roof of the tree-hole. Bramley slowly followed her gaze and eyed directly above himself. There, hanging from the roof were ninety chrysalises, all huddled together, all made up of beautiful rainbow colours, all quiet and still.

"They're sleeping and dreaming now," whispered Bee. "They're all asleep and I'll be joining them soon," she smiled at Bramley, "Thank you, Daddy, for looking after us."

Bramley appeared more than a little confused. "But what's happening? What's happening to you'z all?"

Bee reached out and touched Bramley's cheek, gently. She smiled and yawned. "It's our way. We sleep and wake up!" she yawned again. "Don't worry, I'll see you again soon. Watch over my brothers and sisters."

"But...?" Bramley tried to get his words out, but his throat tingled and tightened and a single tear fell from his eye onto Bee's tiny hand.

Her hand closed around the tear and she pulled her arms into her body. She smiled one last time at Bramley, then her eyes closed and her body cuddled up and a golden blanket encased her. Then she slept.

Bramley sat anxiously on the edge of the tree hole looking out across the fields. Darkness was crawling across the fields like an unstoppable rolling wave, fighting the light of the rising half-moon. His mind was running jam-packed, filled up with thoughts of all that had happened that day.

He thought about how the Dragonflyers had entered his home and destroyed it. What were they looking for, and why? Was it the golden pollen? No, it couldn't be, it was secret and the secret was safe with the Queen...'

"No, it's mee'z!" Bramley mumbled to himself, "They're looking for mee'z! If they find mee'z, they find the children. They found my'z house, so they must know, I'z hiding the children. But how is that possible? And if they found my'z house and they're looking for mee'z, it won't be long before they find the tree. The TREE..! I'z have to move away from here. Quickly! I'z have to move them. I'z have to move them tonight!"

It was then that Bramley recalled that he had seen an empty timeworn human house situated across the meadows, not that far from the old tree.

It would be a long night taking all the children's chrysalises across the fields to the house, but it would be just like carrying buckets of pollen to the hive which he did every day at work. He would need to carry four at a time and there was a half-moon and clear skies to help him see.

Bramley carefully took down the first four of the hanging chrysalises from the tree hole and started out towards the human house. He used the moon's light to navigate his way.

Finally, arriving at the house, Bramley flew all around it, looking for a promising way to enter. He first tried the chimney, but there was a strong draught coming out of it, whistling upwards, much too strong for him to fly against.

The house was boarded up and the glass impenetrable. There appeared to be no holes big enough for him to crawl through. Eventually, Bramley spotted a pipe coming out of the wall under the thatched roof. It was just big enough for him to scramble his way through.

Dragging the chrysalises behind him, he managed to crawl through the pipe and finally appear out of the other end, into the loft of the house. It was dark but he could see all around him, and most importantly, it was warm and dry.

Perfect! he thought to himself. He tied the four chrysalises using some sticky silk, which he found attached to the ends to the straw-thatched ceiling.

Bramley gazed around the loft. There was no other way in except through the pipe. He immediately started to crawl his way back through and then set off again to fetch the next batch of children.

5.

The light behind the hills in the east began to brighten as the dawn began to rise and Bramley finally hung the last of the chrysalises in the loft of the old human house. He was now totally exhausted and hungry and wanted so much to sleep. He looked carefully up at the chrysalises all hanging peacefully together and finally, for the first time that night, felt safety all around him.

"I'z better count you'z again, just to make sure you'z all here," Bramley said, speaking out loud, "Before I'z fall sleep... Ninety!" he counted exactly, then yawning heavily, he repeated the number again, "Ninety." Then he said it gently once last time... "Ninety..."

Snappishly, he opened his eyes, rapidly realising there was one baby missing.

"Bee! I'z left Bee! She wasn't with the others; she was hanging on the other side of the tree hole. How stupid of mee'z!" he scolded himself.

Bramley's whole body ached as he inched his way back up through the pipe. He was extremely drained and weak from having carried all the other children throughout the night, but the thought of leaving Bee behind made him fight the pain.

Eventually, he arrived back at the tree. The sun had just started to appear at the other end of the valley like a small diamond peeping through the gap between the hills; gradually growing bigger and bigger, its yellow haze bringing everything to life.

Suddenly, Bramley heard a strange noise, what sounded like fast beating wings coming from above. He glared up and was instantly terrified to see the dark silhouette of a Dragonflyer, circling the tree.

He hurriedly took cover under a large green leaf and watched as the Dragonflyer swiftly swooped down and landed on a nearby branch, its body rippled through in greens and blacks. It was breathing heavily; the Dragonflyer's green eyes had red pupils, which flicked and skimmed from side to side, as its head moved instantly in the direction of the slightest sound.

Abruptly it raised itself up off the branch, its long legs dangling with its spiny claws, and headed in the direction of the cavity cut into the trunk, cautiously hovering around, dodging the leaves. Bramley had to act fast. He spotted an old dead twig sticking out of the branch. He grabbed at it and pulled it hard. It bent. Bramley pulled harder. "Break," he muttered angrily to himself. Then, with a sudden snap, the twig snapped and fell towards the ground.

The Dragonflyer instantly heard the clatter and turned hastily around and flew to where the snapping sound had come from. At the same time, Bramley flew around the back of the tree and up towards the hole. He stared down the length of the trunk to see the Dragonflyer now flying low towards the ground, following the sound of the tumbling twig as it hit the branches below.

Bramley quickly entered the hole and was immediately overcome by the darkness that hit him. He desperately strained to see where he was going. Using his memory, he headed to where he remembered Bee was hanging.

There she was, exactly where he had left her. Bramley grabbed at her pod her with all his arms and pulled, but the silk holding her was strong. He pulled again, but all his strength had been used up. He put his feet against the wall of the tree and pushed and pulled. Suddenly, Bee's chrysalis broke free and he fell against the floor holding Bee in his arms.

Outside of the tree hole, the Dragonflyer materialized again drifting in an up-and-down cautious wave, as though trying to see into the darkness of the hole.

Bramley instantly froze, lying still on the floor, not daring to breathe. The Dragonflyer momentarily disappeared, moving away from the entrance to the hole. Bramley soundlessly got up and went over to take a look. Still holding Bee in his arms, he watched as the Dragonflyer flew around to the back of the tree. Instantly seizing his chance, Bramley exited the cavity and clung frantically to the underside of the thick branch.

It might have been a mistake, as the Dragonflyer rapidly materialised and settled for a moment on the topside of Bramley's branch. Then, without warning, two more Dragonflyers appeared and settled onto the same branch. Bramley was terrified!

He could hear them whispering to each other in Dragon tongue. He could also feel his arms growing weaker and weaker. Then, just as quickly as they had appeared on the branch, the three Dragonflyers soared into the tree hole. Bramley could hear their voices resonating from side to side within the hollow and the all-encompassing sound of everything within being destroyed.

At that same moment, Bramley's arms finally failed him and he dropped, falling directly onto the branch below as a dreadful pain shot through his body. And as it did, he inexplicably dropped Bee and she tumbled alone towards the earth below.

Instantaneously, Bramley flew after her, trying to catch up. The ground sped up towards them both as they descended.

Bramley beat his wings harder than he ever had before, trying to close the gap between them, the pain unbearable, the ground heading ever closer towards them, closer and closer. Bramley reached out at a single strand of sticky silk trailing just behind Bee's chrysalis, beating his wings ever harder. He felt the tip of the silk touch his fingers and he grabbed at it.

"Got you!" he gasped, but the ground was fast approaching. He shifted gear into reverse with all his strength, his body shuddering, his muscles squealing and felt the grass whip against his body as he pulled out of the dive, barely missing the earth.

Bramley landed hard against the roots of the tree with Bee in his arms and stared back up at the tree. The Dragonflyers were still inside.

Breathing desperately, heavily, he immediately took off again, his entire body racked in pain, and headed towards the safety of the house.

Gently, Bramley pulled Bee through the pipe to safety, struggling to unearth the last of his strength to fly up to the wooden beam in the roof to suspend her next to her siblings in the thatch. He very carefully tied a knot with the remaining silk, his small arms weak and heavy, his energy exhausted.

As he did, he faintly breathed out and toppled backwards, his arms stretched out as if to grab and hold the now invisible Bee in his arms. Bramley's eyesight faded and his eyes slowly closed, as he fell into the darkness below.

6.

On the edge of the forest, across the far side of the valley from the old tree, a figure stood observing.

"They have gone, my Queen," a voice belonging to Lord Redwing, the Queen's Chief Henchman, apologised, "We have searched everywhere."

"Keep looking. Find them!" came the shrill reply.

7.

As the day progressed, Lord Redwing and his soldiers set up watch over the beehive Bramley Bee owed his allegiance to, along with its old Queen.

"Are they in place?" he demanded of his Lieutenant.

"Yes, my lord, they're all in place. We're ready.
We just await your signal, my lord."

"Is the Bee inside, my lord?"

"I don't know," replied Redwing, "But all Bees run to their Queen. If he is inside, bring him out to me alive; if he's not there, then find out where he's hiding. Once inside, go straight for the Queen. She and the King are both old and weak. Investigate and discover the information our Queen demands and then destroy the hive. Leave nothing alive. The Bees must not hear our approach, must not hear a thing, so strike before sunrise. Do not give them a chance to organize and communicate. Now go. Prepare and strike before dawn. They should all still be sleeping in their cozy little nest!"

8.

"You'z Majesty! You'z Majesty! We'z under attack from Dragonflyers!" came the shocked voice of the Guard Bee as he flew into the Queen's chamber. "They've broken into the main hall and are destroying everything!"

The Queen contemplated silently for a moment, standing next to her husband, and then turned calmly towards the Guard.

"Send out the signal to the Hornets and then get everyone out to the forest. Make a path to lead the Dragonflyers directly to me."

"But, you'z Majesty!" the Guard Bee answered in a quarrelsome manner.

"Go'z immediately!" ordered the Queen in a stern, beleaguered voice.

The Guard looked at them both, realising that neither of them intended to leave. He tried arguing one last time, "But, you'z Majesties, I'z you'z Royal Guard. I'z cannot possibly leave you'z both here unprotected."

The Queen moved towards him and pushed an envelope into his hand. "Take this immediately to my'z daughter. It'z vital she receives it. Guard it with you'z life! Do not let anyone take it from you'z. Now go, that i'z my final order!"

The Guard knew his duty and departed the chamber. The Queen and King stood alone together in the empty room and the King turned to his wife and smiled, "You'z the most precious light in my life!"

The huge doors suddenly swung open wide and several Dragonflyers burst into the room.

Lord Redwing looked on from outside, watching as the swarm of Bees swiftly exited, rising above the hive, fleeing towards the trees as his Dragonflyers bore down on them. Then suddenly, there came a deep, droning sound. The shadows of unwelcome assailants appeared rapidly overhead and instantly began to fall upon the Dragonflyers.

Redwing quickly stepped back to hide under the cover of a tree branch and hissed, "Hornets!"

9.

"You failed me!" shrieked, Queen Sindeena, whirling towards Redwing, who slowly backed away, his head lowered in humiliation.

The other Dragonflyers, who were crowded around the darkly lit stone circle filled with black lifeless water, hurriedly followed suit. They scuttled backwards into the darkness of the surrounding trees, trying to avoid the wrath of their Queen, leaving only their glowing red eyes peering back through the blackness.

"Your Majesty... They knew we were coming," muttered Redwing, raising his head marginally but not looking directly at his Queen.

Sindeena glowered at Redwing. "Twenty of my subjects killed and nothing to show for it. And nothing from you, but feeble excuses! Where is this one single Bee? How can he possibly hide among so many of those monstrous creatures? Someone must know where he is!" she reiterated, slamming her wooden staff on the ground, its head suddenly glowing a luminescent green from the impact.

Ripples suddenly appeared on the black oily stained pool and disappeared into a central circle with an unpleasant dripping sound.

Redwing stood still and alone in front of his Queen as though a stone statue. Sluggishly, his head lifted and twitched.

"There is one place, my Queen."

Sindeena took a single step forward and bent down, her face ever closer to Redwing, giving him one last chance to redeem himself. Her green eyes were wide and piercing as she glared down on him. "There's a human house, not far from the old tree," said Redwing.

Sindeena stood up and quickly spun round, her back to Redwing.

"A human house?" she whispered.

"Yes, my Queen... We believe it's empty," he added.
"So, why haven't you searched it?" Sindeena demanded, raising her voice and turning back to face Redwing, the green glow again appearing from the top of her staff.

"Bats live there," Redwing murmured feebly, trying to conceal the fear in his voice. Behind him, the voices of the other Dragonflyers in the trees could now be heard.

"Bats... night creatures?'

"Bats?" Sindeena repeated after a moment, "Are you sure?" she asked, glowering at her commander.

"Yes," Redwing said, "they've been seen flying near there."

Sindeena stared down at her dark reflection in the cold black water, as though she could see deep into it.

 "They're there!" she quietly said to herself. Her reflection smiled back up at her. "Send out your scouts immediately to check."

"Now, while it's dark, your Majesty?" asked the unbelieving Lord Redwing.

"Immediately! Bats only hunt at night. Watch where they go exactly to rest once the sun comes up." answered the Queen dismissively.

10.

The sun shining through the leaves; the sound of distant laughter; Dragonflyers' piercing red eyes everywhere; Bee Lady's face smiling and her beautiful coloured wings; green eyes appearing unexpectedly; a scream; rain falling into black water; the colours of the rainbow; and then darkness.

Loss. A dream? A voice in the distance calling, "Bramley, Bramley, wake up!"

A sudden warm feeling engulfed Bramley's body and he slowly became conscious to the sounds and smells around him. In the distance, he could hear the gentle sound of a young girl's voice calling his name.

"Bramley, wake up!" begged the voice.

He sluggishly opened his eyes. Everything appeared dark and fuzzy.

"Bramley!" repeated the voice.

He urgently tried to focus. Slothfully, a gold sun appeared before him, surrounded by a rainbow. He tried to focus even harder and it began to clear; replaced by a face smiling with beautiful coloured wings.

"It's me, Bee!" said the smiling face.

"Bee! Bee Lady?" Bramley said quietly, struggling to work out where he was and what was happening to him. His head was feeling light and disorientated.

"No, it's Bee!" replied the voice.

Bramley carefully sat up, wiped his face with both hands and beheld the beautiful girl sitting next to him. There was something strangely familiar about her, but he couldn't recognise her face at first. "You'z Bee?" he asked, "You'z not Bee, you'z a Butterfly."

Bramley stared at the girl's beautiful wings and then considered her face. Bee put her hands on Bramley's shoulders and looked into his eyes.

"Look at me, Daddy, it's me." She smiled again. "I've woken up! I've changed into a Butterfly. Don't you recognise me, Daddy?"
"Bee, iz it'z really you'z?" Bramley leant forward and hugged Bee. "How long have I'z been asleep?" he asked her.

"I don't know, Daddy. I only awoke a little time ago."

Hurriedly there was what seemed like a thousand voices above him, all shouting, "Daddy!"

Bramley slowly stood up and brushed himself down and then raised his arms to the air. "My'z children, you'z all Butterflies. You'z all safe? You'z all well? What happened?" Bramley asked, as he turned to Bee, "I'z just remember holding you'z, and then suddenly, darkness."

"You saved us, Daddy," Bee said and smiled again.

At that moment, Bramley heard a noise in the darkness, coming from beyond the loft; a heavy, rasping breath and the sound of something cumbersome moving towards him. He turned quickly, with his back to Bee, as though to guard her.

"It's okay," said Bee, grabbing his arm. "It's just a Natterer."

"A Natterer?" Bramley whispered, still feeling an instinct to protect his family.

"Yes," Bee said, "He saved you. He has the answers to all your questions." Suddenly, the noise appeared again and out of the darkness, two white, piercing eyes stared intensely at Bramley. He wanted to step backwards, but instead he took a deep breath. "Show youzself!"

Two long dark legs materialized, stepping clumsily, each with a single, strong claw-like finger on the end with leathery stretched wings attached, followed by a large, rounded body of fur. Its face slowly emerged out of the dark shadows with large ears and a snout. It had a kind face, even though fangs protruded from its mouth. Not exactly what Bramley had imagined. Its huge body seemed uncomfortable resting on the floor. It looked down on Bramley and sniffed into the air.

"You're awake then," it said.

Bramley stood silent next to Bee. He'd never seen a creature like this before. He realised after a moment that he was staring, and not to be rude, he introduced himself.

"Hello, my'z name iz Bramley. I'z a Beez."

The Natterer's Bat moved a little closer, stomping the floor clumsily with one leg.

Bramley continued, "I'z believe you'z have some answers for mee'z."

The Bat looked down at Bee and then again at Bramley. "Yes, your friend here told me your name and who you are," the Bat said, with its deep hoarse voice. "And all your family have told me stories about you. You're lucky!"

"Lucky?" Bramley repeated, "Yez, yez, I'z am, to have this wonderful family."

"No," the Bat glared at him, "You're lucky to be alive!"

"I'z don't understand," said Bramley, "What do you'z mean?"

The Natterer's Bat sniffed and wiped his nose on his bony skeleton-like wing arm, his head and shoulders voluntarily leaning forward nearer to Bramley and Bee.

He spoke gently: "I was here all of last night, hanging high on the beams above in the darkness, when you crawled through the pipe, pulling all those chrysalises after you. At first, I wanted to eat you, but I remembered my father telling me when I was young that yellow flyers like you have a nasty sting. So I decided not to reveal myself and instead watched you.

"You see, I've been trapped in this loft for many nights since the storm. A sudden strong unforeseen wind blew through this human house and the open door in the floor was blown closed and my only escape was sealed, my route to the chimney blocked. I was trapped and alone and my family was outside. They tried to get in but it was hopeless, so I called to them and sent them away. I kept quiet, watching you leave and return many times, and I could hear you talking to each one of the chrysalises as you hung them on the beams, telling them that they were safe now. Each time you returned with more, I could see your strength failing and you getting weaker. But still, you found the power to continue.

"There was something more to you than just determination; something was helping you. I could feel something immensely powerful coming from within you, something emanating around your body. We Bats can feel and see things in ways you could never imagine. I began to admire you. I was going to reveal myself but I decided to wait. All through the night you worked, until finally you brought this last little one here by herself."

The Bat looked at Bee and then continued, "She was the last, but you were done, totally broken. You were dying! I watched as you fell. But as you did, a cloud of light like a rainbow came from within your body. It was so bright; I was blinded for a moment, absolutely taken by surprise. I flew towards you to try to catch you, but the light was too strong and I missed you." The Natterer sniffed and wiped his nose again, then continued, "You were lucky!"

Bramley stepped a little closer to Bee. Adjacent to his shoulder, he noticed that his entire family of Butterflies had come down from the loft quietly and were encircling them just like they did when they were baby caterpillars, listening intently to the story.

"A light? Lucky?" Bramley repeated, "Why was I'z lucky and what light?"

The Natterer's Bat smiled again and continued to speak. "Light that came from within your body; only you have the answer to that question. You landed on a spider's web. Lucky! The spider's web broke your fall and saved you. But your fall into the web alerted Steatoda, and she was quickly upon you, ready to take you and drag you to her hole. But I was even quicker and confronted her. The light made her hesitate and she backed away."

"Wait," said Bramley, "Who is Steatoda?"

"I am Steatoda!" came a voice from the dark. Everyone turned quickly to face the source. The young Butterflies all gasped with shock and fear at hearing the sudden sound and flew rapidly back up to safety of the rafters, their wings drumming, causing a gentle breeze in the loft, making swirls of dust from the floor rise up. Bramley stood his ground, but ushered Bee behind him. Now he stood in front of Bee and the Natterer's Bat. The dust continued to swirl around, blocking their vision for a moment. It slowly began to settle, and as it did, it revealed Steatoda standing right in front of them.

Bramley felt Bee's hand squeeze his arm; not this time for reassurance, but out of fear.

The spider was standing before them, her reddish legs still and silent, and eight black eyes staring directly at them, close enough for them to see their own reflections. "Don't worry," she replied in an unreassuringly slow, smooth, calculated way. "I... we... have made a deal not to... harm you... with the Bat. I'm more interested in where you... found your light, Bee? I could use a light like that."

Bramley knew of spiders and knew they couldn't be trusted, but at that moment, he wanted answers. He stood his ground. "I'z don't know about any light," he replied.

Suddenly, in a quick but silent scurrying action, Steatoda moved to her left, keeping her eyes on Bramley, and stopped just as abruptly.

"It's there in your chest," she said as her thin, spindly leg rose upwards as though to point.

Bramley put his hand on his chest and felt in his fur. At first, he felt nothing, but then he felt a small object embedded in his skin. It was sticky to touch. He looked down much closer and there he saw the missing piece of gold pollen he thought he had lost from his pocket. It had got stuck with honey in his fur, but it had grown and now resembled a small golden crystal, but more worrying was the fact that it had grown into his body, into his chest.

Bee stared at the pollen crystal. Her eyes widened and sparkled with flashes of green. There was something meaningful in this to her. She wanted to touch it, but resisted.

"It's wonderful!" she whispered.

Bramley put his hand over the crystal. "How do I get it out?

What shall I do?"

Steatoda moved a little closer, but the Natterer's Bat shuffled forward and Steatoda backed away. She muttered, "I can help you take it out... I have some venom that would numb the pain and I could remove it for you... I could help you!"

Again, the Natterer's Bat moved forward and again Steatoda moved backwards, but this time he spoke. "Now is not the time for this, Bramley... It seems to me that whatever it is that made the light, also saved you and gave you the strength to live. But right now, we have more important things to worry about. We need to find a way out. I can sense there are other forces around us. Something is not right and I fear there is danger coming."

Bee, Bramley, the entire Butterfly family and even Steatoda had stopped talking to listen to the Bat. They all started thinking of what the answer might be as to how to get out of the loft, when all of a sudden the Natterer's Bat became agitated and started moving around, mumbling to himself, before promptly and without warning, he stretched his wings and flew very quickly to the top of the loft ceiling and started to make strange clicking noises, flying erratically in wonky zig-zags through the darkness.

"What's wrong with him?" whispered Bee into Bramley's ear, as they both tried to follow his flight. But not such a quiet whisper that Steatoda couldn't hear.

"He's listening to something," she said as she too peered upwards, "I've watched him do this before many times."

After a moment, the Bat landed again on the floor. He sneezed loudly as he came to rest in front of Bramley and Bee, letting loose, a spray of phlegm through the air, which mostly went onto everyone's faces. "That's disgusting," Steatoda gasped, wiping gluey globules from her face.

Natterer wiped his nose again, oblivious to what he had done. Instead, he breathed in deeply; his chest rattled as though he was about to sneeze again. Everyone turned away and covered their faces. The Bat looked at them for a moment, wondering what they were doing.

"There was something outside," he said, looking around at everyone standing with their backs to him. Slowly, they turned and faced him, expecting another soaking. There was an awkward silence for a moment as though an apology was expected, but none came. The Bat repeated what he had said, but this time elaborated: "There was something outside. I could hear them and feel their presence. I think they're Dragonflyers! There were at least five of them. They are watching this human house. It's very strange; I've never sensed them before during the night. They have left now."

11.

Throughout the night the Dragonflyer scouts had been observing the uninhabited human house where the hairy heads had once lived, probing it to see if there were any indications or clues as to the whereabouts of Bramley or his Butterflies. There had been no sign of any Bats flying in and out or near the house, and now the sun was rising steadily into the blue sky.

"We must report back to the Queen," said the lead scout, signalling to the others. They quickly grouped back together and headed back towards the hills and the distance forest.

12.

Bramley sat slumped on the floor feeling downhearted. Bee knelt down beside him, "What's wrong, Daddy? Are you ill?"

"No'z," said Bramley. He gazed around at everyone's faces. "They're looking for uz," he said solemnly. He then briefly retold the story of his escape from the tree; how his home had been destroyed, and how the Dragonflyers were trying to find both him and his children.

He told them all about Bee Lady and the promise he had made her, as well as about the golden pollen she had left him to care for them. He now realised that it had far more magical powers than he had first thought.

Bee stroked Bramley's head, "It's okay, Daddy. We're safe in here."

Bramley looked into Bee's eyes. He could now clearly see her mother, Bee Lady, in her face. He thought of the promise he had made to her, to protect Bee and her siblings.

"No'z," said Bramley abruptly, standing up and regaining his resolve. "We'z haz to escape and get out of here, now! We have no'z food and no'z water and the Dragonflyers will be back and will find uz eventually. We'll be'z trapped."

"And how do you suppose to do that?" snapped Steatoda, "As I see it, only you and I can fit through that pipe." She then hesitated a moment, thinking, then added, "Together we could escape... and yes... you and I could get help?"

"No'z," exclaimed Bramley, "We'z all going to get out of here together, there has to be a way!"

"The only way out is through the door in the floor," said the Bat.

Bramley looked once again into the faces of his ninety-one children. They all stared at him for reassurance. He considered the Bat for a moment, which was looking a touch discouraged. He finally turned and looked at Steatoda. She was preening her legs, scraping away strands of her silk web.

"Steatoda?" Bramley said, watching her go through the motions of discarding the silk, "Your silk iz strong, izn't it?"

She immediately stopped, glared back at Bramley and smiled. "It's strong enough to tie a Bat to the ground," she said looking across at the Natterer.

The Bat turned back towards the spider, and showed her his fangs and teeth, his face instantly screwed up and distorted.

"The same way my teeth could cut you in half," he replied, glaring at her. "Wait," said Bramley, "Now iz not the time to fight amongst ourselves, we'z need each other. Show mee'z the door in the floor. I'z have an idea."

The Bat then showed Bramley and the others, as they congregated around the spot containing a door in the floor.

"We can't lift it. It looks far too heavy," said Bee.

Bramley smiled back at her. "Steatoda, we'z going to need your strong silk," Bramley then said, moving towards her, "Can you'z make ninety-three strands of silk and attach them to the door?"

"I could spin my silk all day, but it will take some time to make that many."

"Good," said Bramley, "Get started now and give a strand to each of my'z children when it'z tied to the door. You need to make each strand long enough to reach the beam above!"

Bee and the rest of the Butterflies instantly, excitedly, started chatting amongst themselves. Realising what Bramley had in mind, the Bat spoke with caution, "You want to try to lift the door using the silk? It won't be strong enough. We are not strong enough."

Bramley looked at Natterer, "Do you'z remember watching mee'z bringing in all these children through the night? I'z did it because I had to. I'z found the strength. You'z, mee'z and the Butterflies, we'z will find the strength. We'z do it! We'z only need to lift it'z a little to get through!"

13.

Deep in the forest, in its darkest furthermost place, where the sun was barely visible through its thick foliage, which just allowed enough scattered beams of light through to strike the damp, moss-ridden surface which gave little visibility, its ground strewn with rotting tree limbs covered in yellow, sickly looking funguses, stood Sindeena, close to the black pool of oily stagnant water, talking to her own reflection.

"Yes, my sister, the time is near. We shall have..."

All of a sudden, her scouts returned, settling on a rock close by. Sindeena stopped mid-sentence. "Well, what news do you bring me?" she demanded.

One of the scouts stepped forward, his head moving around, turning on its side as though cowering. "We saw no one, your Majesty. No Bats, no creatures. It was quiet," he said, bowing his head lower.

Sindeena looked across at Redwing.

"Prepare my Dragonflyers. We leave for the human house. They're in there hiding. I know it! We must go now, before they move again."

14.

It was getting late. Steatoda had been spinning her silk all day and now she had just finished creating her ninety-third silk strand. She was tired, but the job was finally completed.

"I'm exhausted," she said, as Bramley thanked her and took the last strand of silk web and flew up to the loft ceiling.

All the Butterflies were perched along the wooden beam. Bee was standing with her brothers and sisters and the Natterer's Bat was balancing precariously, using his wings to steady his bony legs.

"On my'z signal," Bramley shouted, "We'z all take the strain and pull the web tight. Then on my'z second signal, we'z all fly, one by one, over and under the beam, pulling the silk around the beam."

Just at the moment Bramley was about to signal, Steatoda appeared, swinging through the air and landing on the thatching next to the Natterer's Bat.

"Here," she said, dangling in front of him, "Take this. It's double-strength silk. I wouldn't want yours to break and then you blame me for his crazy idea not working."

The Bat smiled at her.

"If this works, we'll have stories to tell our children," said Steatoda.

"We're ready!" shouted the Natterer.

Bramley held his silk strand, "Take the strain," he called, and everyone clenched tight on their silks. "Pull!" shouted Bramley, "Pull!!"

There was a sudden creaking sound as the door in the floor lifted slightly. A shaft of light appeared along the opening, and then a gush of wind sucked back through the gap that had appeared, pulling the door back harshly on itself.

"Pull harder!!!" shouted Bramley. The door slowly crept open again, the draught sucking at it, trying to wrench it back. Bramley suddenly shouted, "Fly, fly now!"

The Natterer's Bat flapped his wings and rose into the air, followed shortly by Bee, then one by one, the rest of the Butterflies took off, taking the strain and beating their wings, all ninety-one of them. The noise was incredible. They all dropped around the back of the beam, pulling the silk tauter.

The door creaked again and the air gushed out. The door rose sluggishly this time, the air now working for them, pushing it up.

"It'z working!" Bramley cried out, "Fly harder!" The door rose a little higher. "Tie the silk around the beam," he shouted. They all flew harder. Circling around whilst reaching out to wrap their silk ends firmly around the solid beam, the little Butterflies finally managed to tie their silks around the thick wood.

Steatoda quickly scurried down the lengths of silk strands, weaving more silk thread between them, strengthening them and forming a massive web.

"Bee," Bramley called out, "lead everyone out through the door."

Bee flew down to the opening and floated in the entranceway while she ushered each of her siblings through the gap. The Natterer landed with a bump on the floor, next to Bee, shortly followed by Bramley.

"I knew it would work!" the Bat said, smiling at Bramley.

They both looked through the gap to the room below, where the other Butterflies were now flying around.

"We'z must go. I'z not sure this web will hold much longer. This through draught iz very strong," said Bramley.

The Natterer turned and looked back into the attic. "It was a good home," he said. He then saw Steatoda, still spinning her web. He shouted up to her, "Spider, you must leave. It won't hold."

She stopped and stared back down at them. "I'm not leaving," she shouted, "This is my home. I told you my silk is strong enough to tie a Bat down, so it can hold an old door open! Don't forget, we still have a deal, so go."

Bramley looked back at the Bat. "What deal?"

The Bat shrugged his shoulders. Bramley turned and shouted up to thank Steatoda, and bid her farewell and good luck. Then Bee, Bramley and the Bat slipped through the door.

15.

Outside the human house, Sindeena had gathered her Dragonflyers and positioned some of them in the trees, some in the long grass surrounding the house, and some lying in wait on the thatched roof.

It was getting late and the sun was already starting to set over the hills in the distance. The summer light was fading and the cool breeze flowing across the tall grass was getting stronger.

Sindeena was standing alone on the corner of the roof when Lord Redwing landed and settled next to her. He was about to speak when Sindeena raised her hand. "Shhh, quiet! Can you hear that?"

Redwing listened. Suddenly, a sound came resonating through the thatch, a muffled sound of wings beating hard. Sindeena chuckled to herself, "They're in there! They're moving!"

"There's only one way out, my Queen," said Redwing. "The chimney," he said, pointing to the top of the house.

"Go!" she said, "Take your men and wait. I want my sister alive. Kill the rest."

Redwing flew up to hover over the chimney taking some of the Dragonflyers with him.

Sindeena flew down to the side of the house to see if she could see inside, holding her staff tightly in both hands.

Instantly she recognised the voice coming from directly behind her.

"You didn't think I would leave my daughter alone and unprotected did you, sister?"

Sindeena froze. The wind caught her hair and blew it sideward, green strands shimmering in the last rays of the sunset, her long green dress flapping in the breeze, the green glow slowly emanating from the top of her staff. She raised her head and glared up at the top of the house, her back still to Bee Lady.

"Daughter..?" she whispered to herself. "Ha," she laughed, whirling around, "You're too late, Belliza!" she yelled, training her staff directly at Bee Lady.

"It's been a long time, sister. Or, are you really my sister? My sister died a long time ago. You are an abomination!" Sindeena hissed.

Bee Lady gently and gracefully flapped her wings. Her body was silhouetted against the last throes of light, showed their worn and ageing edges.

"You know exactly who I am!" answered Belliza. "Yes, I am your sister and I have come to collect my daughter in order for her to fulfil her destiny."

"There will be no destiny!" Sindeena hissed, at the same time lunging her staff towards Bee Lady.

16.

Bramley, Bee, and all the Butterflies followed Natterer through the empty house. They finally came to a room with a hole in the wall, which the hairy heads called a fireplace.

The Natterer Bat led the way. Stopping just in front of the fireplace, he turned to Bramley. "There's a strong up-draught. You don't need to fly, just let the wind pull you up."

The young Butterflies looked nervous and afraid and all started to voice their concerns. Quickly, Bee flew to the front and faced them. "Don't worry, my brothers and sisters, I'm sure it's safe." She looked at Bramley and smiled. "I'll go first!"

"Wait!" said Bramley.

But before he could say another word, Natterer spoke, "It'll be okay, Bramley. I'll follow her. You stay here and make sure your children all come up after us."

"I'll come to the window when I'm through and show you I'm alright," reassured Bee.

Bee then stepped backwards into the mouth of the fireplace; her wings quickly ruffled in the wind and her feet lifted off the ground, and in a whisper she was gone.

The Bat then hobbled into the mouth of the fireplace and turned to Bramley, smiling.

"Don't worry, she'll be okay." Then suddenly, his face changed. It rapidly contorted into a snarl. Shadows appeared on the wall above the fireplace. Bramley switched his gaze from the Bat to the shadows.

Two shadowy forms on the wall were embraced in a struggle. One was a Butterfly, one was a... Bramley turned around quickly. There, through the window, he saw Bee Lady. She was besieged by what seemed to be a Dragonfly, holding a long wooden staff.

Bramley instantly flew across to the window, his hands pressed up against the pane of glass. He watched helplessly as two more Dragonflyers came up behind Bee Lady and grabbed her wings. He watched in horror as the Dragonflyers pulled Bee Lady to the ground. Frozen in shock, all Bramley could do was scream, "No!"

17.

Bee was propelled up the dark chimney. She looked constantly upwards as the light at the end came ever closer and closer. Suddenly, with a burst of energy from the draught, she was released into the open sky, directly into the clutches of Lord Redwing.

"I have someone who wants to see you, Bee Lady," Redwing murmured into Bee's ear, as he held her tightly, pulling her higher into the darkening sky, Bee tried to struggle, but Redwing was too powerful. "I know she has something special in mind for you."

Just at that moment, a sudden jolt sent Bee tumbling out of control into a free fall and a loud shriek of pain came from Redwing, as Natterer Bat intentionally collided at full speed into him, sending them both spinning through the air.

Inside, Bramley flew away from the window towards the fireplace; his mind in total shock, first at seeing Bee Lady, and then at the thought of her likely imminent demise. As he did, he beckoned to his Butterfly family to follow. "We'z must get out, now. Follow mee'z!" he said, not knowing what could be waiting for them outside, but knowing it would be better to fly and try to escape, rather than being trapped inside the house.

Bramley sped up the chimney and burst into the sky. A full moon greeted him, rising above the solitary tree. He quickly looked around, to see the sky was full of Dragonflyers circling overhead. He saw Bee lying on the roof of the house and flew down to her. "Are you'z hurt?" he said as he landed next to her.

"No, I'm all right," she said, "I'm just a bit winded."

"Bee, you'z must go. Lead you'z brothers and sisters away from here. Go now!"

At that moment, the first Butterflies flew out of the chimney, heading straight towards the Dragonflyers' trap above.

Bee looked on in desperation, quickly realising the impending slaughter of her family was about to begin, when all of a sudden, a loud clicking sound entered her ears, and Natterer Bat shot rapidly past them directly upwards towards the Dragonflyers.

He was instantly followed by two more Bats, and then another two, shadowed by two more. There was now a massive sound of clicking all around them. Natterer shouted down, "We'll clear the path, Bee."

"Go, Bee. Lead them to safety," Bramley said. He grabbed Bee and hugged her. "Go, my'z daughter," he said, kissing her on her cheek and then pushed her away, "Go, now!"

Bee stared at Bramley. "What? Where are you going?"

"I'z have to do something. I'z have to go now. Go now, please," he repeated, "Take care of my'z children." Bramley then suddenly turned and was gone.

As he flew over to the side of the house, he could see Bee Lady in the grass, being held down by the Dragonflyers.

Standing in front of her was the one who he guessed had to be

Sindeena. She was old and worn, her face wrinkled and full of hate, her staff positioned to strike at Bee Lady. He had to stop her.

Then from nowhere, with a powerful blow, a sharp dagger hit Bramley in the back. The pain shot through his entire body. His breath stopped and he fell back against the wall of the house. He just managed to turn to see his attacker. Lord Redwing hovered over him, his face torn and cut, his wings shredded.

"You won't escape me this time, Bee," he hissed, readying himself to plunge a finishing blow into Bramley. But before he could, there was an enormous loud clicking and a dark shadow appeared above.

Again, Natterer Bat smashed into Redwing and they went tumbling in a deathly embrace into the dense grass.

Bramley breathed in. The pain quickly subsided, but everything around him seemed to have slowed down. He glared into the sky above.

Butterflies, Bats and Dragonflyers were contorted in a slow dance of death. He felt totally helpless; he had failed to protect the ones he loved. He looked around and spotted Sindeena, raising her arms to strike a deadly blow down on Bee Lady, when in the distance he saw what he first thought to be a dark cloud approaching them. Then he realised his mistake. Moving at great speed towards them was the ever-increasing droning sound of a thousand swarming Bees.

Bramley thrust himself away from the wall and sped over towards Sindeena. Everything instantly became clearer, including the evil Queen. He saw her force the staff into Bee Lady's chest, whilst screaming at her, "Give me the crystals!"

Bramley yelled, "No'zll!"

Bee Lady instantly fell backwards. Sorrow, pain and above all anger filled Bramley's soul at that precise moment and he immediately turned his body and sting in the direction of Sindeena.

As he sped towards her, she quickly turned around, sensing his approach. She raised her staff one more time, ready to swipe at Bramley, laughing and shouting madly, "Stupid Bee!"

However, a sudden lightning bolt shock of coloured light sprang like a laser from Bramley's chest, directly into Sindeena's eyes. She screeched and Bramley's sting struck at the very centre of her heart.

Sindeena stood for a moment statue-like, with her mouth wide open wide as though to scream, but no sound emitted from her throat. Stunned, her eyes blackened and her arms flung fully open as she toppled backwards.

"Yes, they're all safe. They all got away."

"And Bee?"

"Yes, I'm okay," came a voice, as Bee suddenly appeared, resting up next to Bramley.

Bee Lady looked up at Bee. "My'z daughter?" she asked in a whisper.

Bee looked at Bramley, he nodded. "This iz you'z mother, Bee."

"My child. This is not how I wanted you to meet me. I'm so sorry. I knew Sindeena would try to find you, so I tried to leave a false trail. I left you with Bramley. He was the only one I trusted." Her voice began to falter.

Bee Lady put her hands into her pockets and brought out shining gold pollen crystals and placed them into Bee's hands. They glowed momentarily. "You must put them in your dress pockets and keep them there. Do not take them out. Place buddleia pollen with them, until the new moon appears. They are your future and your past memories; they are the last ones."

Bee Lady turned to face Bramley, "You look tired, Bramley. You're pale."

The Queen Bee stared at Bramley. "Bramley, where's you'z sting?" she asked.

Bramley looked back over his shoulder to where he had last seen Sindeena.

"It'z in the proper place, you'z Majesty" he said, turning back to look at the new Queen.

Bee Lady knew straight away what this meant to a Bee.

"What have you done, Bramley? Why...?"

Bramley smiled down at Bee Lady. "For our children, my'z lovely."

Tears fell from Bee's face as she suddenly realised she was about to lose both her father and her mother. She looked down gently at Bee Lady.

"Mother, take back the pollen. Use them to save yourselves."

Bee Lady shook her head and replied, "It's too late, my daughter. Once they have been placed in my bloodline's hands, they are tied only to them."

Bee Lady then looked up to the sky above, where the full moon now shone down. Her hand touched Bramley's chest where his heart was. There, to her surprise, a light of many colours faintly appeared through

Bramley's fur. She looked at Bramley with sudden intrigue in her eyes.

"What's this?" she said, pushing the fur away, revealing the crystal on his chest.

The light was weak and fading. Bramley explained how it had got there and the part it had played in saving him. Bee Lady looked up again at the moon and then turned to Bee.

"There's still chance for us, to save us, to save your father!"
Bee rose up quickly, as did the Natterer Bat and the Queen.

"What do you mean? How?" she implored her mother.

"You must get us to the hills. There's a lake with a waterfall," Bee Lady replied softly, "We must get there before the moon goes down."

The Natterer Bat gently picked up Bee Lady, and Bee steadied her father, who was growing weaker by the moment.

The Queen Bee told them to go, but that unfortunately she could not help. She had to take care of her Bees and lead them back to the safety of the hive through the night. The Natterer signalled to his family by clicking, "Don't worry," he said, "My family will guide you through the forest. You'll be safe."

The Queen bowed her head.

"You'z a brave Bee, Bramley. You'z a hero," and with that, she sped away.

*****

After a time, Bee, Bramley and Natterer, still carrying Bee Lady, arrived at the lake.

"Over there!" Bee Lady pointed, "Put us down there by those rocks near the waterfall."

The Natterer did as he was asked. Bee Lady again looked up at the moon, "There's still a little time, but we have to be quick."

Bee was so sad and emotional that she clung to her father, not wanting to let him go. "Why are we here, Mother?" she asked.

Bee Lady managed to sit up, leaning against a rock for support, "It's the only way, my child. You must be brave."

Bee Lady beckoned to Bramley. He moved over to her, managing to hover by her side.

"Do you think you can carry me, Bramley?" she asked, smiling at him.

"I would carry you'z to the moon, if you'z asked it of me," he replied. He then gently lifted Bee Lady into his arms.

Bee came over, still not understanding. She put her arms around Bramley and her mother, and sobbed, "Please don't die."

Bee Lady put her hand on Bee's cheek and wiped away her tears.

"This is not the end. This is just another door. You'll understand in time."

Bee Lady and Bramley looked over at the Bat, whose eyes were full of tears. They both nodded to him, and he moved gently forward and put his wing around Bee.

"Take care of my'z little girl and all my'z children," said Bramley. He leant forward and kissed Bee on her forehead. A single tear trickled down Bramley's face, and then he lifted into the air.

"So, where do we'z go, my'z Queen?" asked Bramley.

The full moon slowly drifted, its beams reflecting on the still water. Gently, it positioned itself behind the waterfall's fine spray. As it did, a moon rainbow appeared and arched through the waterfall, disappearing into the depths of the lake.

"There!" Bee Lady pointed at the rainbow, "Fly into the rainbow." Bramley gathered the very last of his strength and flew into the colours, and Bee Lady hugged Bramley closer as he did. She gazed at him and smiled, "My'z Bee!" she whispered.

Bramley kissed her, and as he did, a second rainbow shone out brightly from his chest, its colours instantly mixing together with the moon rainbow.

The colours totally surrounded them both, engulfing them, and then their bodies melted away, together in stars of coloured light. The rainbow then tailed away slowly with the moon into the lake and was gone.

Bee and Natterer both stood in silence, tears streaming down their faces, amazed at what they had just witnessed. After a moment, Bee turned to Natterer: "Take me home."

18.

A solitary moth flew high over the lake, its wings flapping erratically as moths' wings do. It circled for a moment and then dropped to the surface, where the rainbow's end had been. The moth then seemed to bounce on the water and then flutter away.

The view from above revealed in the deep dark water, the glow of a crystal stone.

****

They dragged Sindeena back into the depths of the forest.
Her body now lay next to the black pool, one of her hands half submerged.

Her staff lay next to her, and a single ripple sluggishly floated across its surface.

****

The story now ends, or does it? Blackness is all around, and for a moment there's nothing. Just quiet.

19.

Suddenly, a speck of gold appears in the darkness and gets larger and larger.

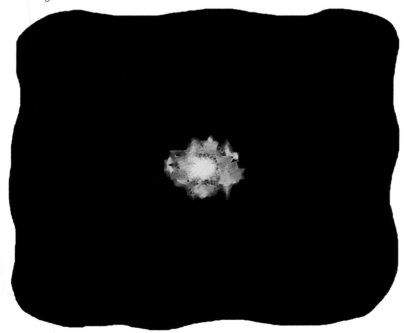

A swirl of colour, a world of rainbows, gold hills and mountains appear, followed by a rainbow-blue lake with a gushing rainbow waterfall, surrounded with rocks and glowing flowers.

Two faint opaque spheres with sparkling gold stars and rainbows twirling inside emerge near to the rocks, and gradually start forming shapes. One the shape and figure of a Butterfly; the other, a Bee.

After a moment, Bramley and Bee Lady materialize, their bodies transparent, but moving. Both gaze down at their own bodies in amazement, and then they look at each other and smile.

Bramley begins to sing to Bee Lady. And as he does, his body changes furthermore. His features slowly transform and he appears more like a Fairy Prince; his wings widen and grow full of colour, like those of a Butterfly, but he keeps his Bee-like presence. They touch hands and Bramley sings:

I see you through the lights
You're here with me
Can you see
I hear your voice
You're close to me

Bee Lady sings:

It's our time
We are free
Come closer
Come next to me
Take my'z hand
Reach out
And bee part of me
You know me
It's really me
You're still you
I know you
We're still the same
You and me
Our minds still remain

Bramley looks down again at his new body, arms and legs and sings:

I feel the light
It's all around
It feels so nice
I can hold your hand
Our lives are here
Our world is now
And I can see you clear
you're really here

They both fly up into the air to behold their new world.

I never thought this would happen to me
I never thought this would happen to us
This is new
This is magic
This is us
This is great
This is magic
Look at us

This is real
...and I'm here with you

They both fly off into the distant rainbow clouds, singing together:

I'm still me
You're still you
We've not changed
...Well not that much
This is magic
This is nuts
This is fun
Take my'z hand
Our lives have just begun

THE END

Ig Oliver

Writing has always been a hobby and cathartic experience for Ig.
Turning his passion into a fulfilling career as a professional author
has been one of his greatest life achievements.

Born in rural Northamptonshire in the 60's, Ig moved later to
Derbyshire to finish his studies, starting his working career as
a chef in the surrounding restaurants and hotels.

Later, he moved to London to work for King Hussain of Jordan. He
then moved to Switzerland where he worked at the American Embassy.

America then called and Ig worked in New York, Palm Springs,
Palm Beach, Los Angeles and Hartford, working as a personal chef
for many famous celebrities and politicians.

By the late 90's, Ig was working as House Manager and Executive
Chef at the British Embassy in Moscow, overseeing the catering of
the first State Visit by HM Queen Elizabeth II and later receiving an
award in the Kremlin, presented to him by The Queen.

Ig now puts pen to paper as both an author and illustrator to apply skills
he has kept on his back burner for most of his career. Having produced
many fine oil paintings and portraits in his spare time, Ig now uses these
skills to create his own beautiful illustrations, which help tell the stories
he has conjured-up in his own remarkable imagination.

Coming next from IG Oliver:

Coming soon from Ventorros Press:

The Realm of Smaller Things

by Kent Knowles

Also available from Ventorros Press:

Also available from Ventorros Press: